Caines

*For the little boy who still stands waving on the railway gate.* J.E.

*For Sheena* J.R.

First published in 1993
Text copyright © Jim Edmiston, 1993
Illustrations copyright © Jane Ross, 1993

Printed in Italy
for J.M. Dent & Sons Ltd
Orion House
5 Upper St. Martin's Lane
London WC2 9EA

A catalogue for this book is available from the British Library.

The illustrations for this book were prepared on silk using wax and inks.

# LITTLE EAGLE LOTS OF OWLS

Jim Edmiston

Illustrated by Jane Ross

Dent Children's Books
London

Little Eagle Lots of Owls has his very own cabin high up in the mountains where the eagles fly. When the sun rises in the east, the sky is filled with birdsong. When it sinks in the west, the land lies silent as the stars.

His grandfather, the old chief, said, "Little Eagle Lots of Owls, you have the sharp eyes of the eagle, and you can see many things. But your name is as long as it takes the moon to walk across the sky."

The boy listened carefully to his grandfather, as a log burnt and slipped, sending sparks crackling up into the night.

"I shall call you 'Little Eagle'," said the old chief, "but you must never forget your true name."

Then one morning, just as the sun began to warm Little Eagle's sleepy face, he received a gift from his grandfather. Little Eagle thanked his grandfather, but then he frowned. What was it? It was a strange creature — a very strange creature.

It did not have the soft fur of the rabbit or the hard scales of the lizard. It was not big, but it was not small. It had no top and it had no tail.

It was impossible to tell which side was the back and which was the front. No ears, eyes, nose, or mouth could be seen. But it snored. It was fast asleep.

Little Eagle prodded it, but it kept on sleeping. He stood with it beneath the open sky. The song of the birds could not wake it up.

He took it to the river's edge. The rush of the tumbling water could not wake it up.

He took it to the forest. The bellowing moose could not wake it up.

He took it to the rolling plains. Even the stampeding buffalo could not wake it up.

Little Eagle jumped up and down. He whooped and yelled and beat his drum. His rain-dance only made it rain. When he stopped, the sun shone again, and Little Eagle sat and sat. He shook his head. He had seen many things from his mountain where the eagles fly, but never anything like this.

But as the earth rolled over like a sleeping bear, and the sun went down without a sound at all, the creature stopped snoring. It woke up. It opened its eyes – all six of them. Little Eagle gasped. It was not one creature. It was three fat owls, huddling together.

They beat their wings and filled the darkening sky with their cries.

"Leloo, leloo! Leloo, leloo!"
Little Eagle Lots of Owls laughed and clapped his hands.

On another mountain, the old chief heard the laughter and smiled, as he watched the moon walk slowly across the sky.

"Little Eagle Lots of Owls," he murmured, "you have the sharp eyes of the eagle and you are as wise as the owl. Now you know your true name."